THE MYSTERIOUS WORLD OF

COSENTINO

For my princess ... Priscilla
—COS

For Jeremy Quay, who helped me discover one of
my favorite magicians—Jack Heath

For my three ~~miners~~ minors: Eva, Jesse & Heath
—James Hart

First American Edition 2019
Kane Miller, A Division of EDC Publishing

Text & illustrations copyright © Scholastic Australia, 2019

Text by Cosentino with Jack Heath
Illustrations by James Hart
Published by Scholastic Australia in 2019
Internal images: p2 and various pages, Stars © Alisovna/Creative Market

For information contact:
Kane Miller, A Division of EDC Publishing
PO Box 470663
Tulsa, OK 74147-0663
www.kanemiller.com
www.edcpub.com
www.usbornebooksandmore.com

Library of Congress Control Number: 2018952951

Printed and bound in the United States of America

1 2 3 4 5 6 7 8 9 10

ISBN: 978-1-61067-752-3

THE MYSTERIOUS WORLD OF COSENTINO

THE SILVER THIEF

By **COSENTINO**

THE GRAND ILLUSIONIST

WITH JACK HEATH

ILLUSTRATED BY JAMES HART

Kane Miller
A DIVISION OF EDC PUBLISHING

THE MYSTERIOUS WORLD OF COSENTINO

COPPERTOWN

COSENTINO

Magician at Copperpot Theater
Abilities: Escape, Sleight of hand,
telekinesis, Illusion

LOCKi

Cos's partner at Copperpot Theater
Abilities: Lock picking

NONNA

Prop/costume designer
Copperfield Cottage
Abilities: Healing powers

PROFESSOR CAMOUFLAGE

Celebrity Impersonator at Siegfried Alley
(since escaping from the royal zoo)
Abilities: Can disguise himself as anything

SNUGGLES

Lettuce disposal expert in Cos's hat
Abilities: Appearing and disappearing,
heightened senses

ACE

Former soldier in the Army of 52
Abilities: Transformation

THE MYSTERIOUS WORLD OF COSENTINO

SILVER CITY

HOLLOW

King's Henchman
Abilities: Can smell magic

THE KING OF DIAMONDS

King of Magicland
Abilities: Hypnotism

PRINCESS PRISCILLA

Princess of Magicland
Abilities: Levitation, sweet, kind heart, extremely clever

THE JOKERS

The King's Jesters
Abilities: Naughty, place switchers

SVENGALI VILLAGE

WIGGY

Mine Overseer/Cos's Old Manager
Abilities: Being bossy and cunning

THE MINORS

King's slaves/miners
Silver Mine
Abilities: Being minors

DOVE

King's Silver Layer
Silver Mine
Abilities: Lays eggs of silver

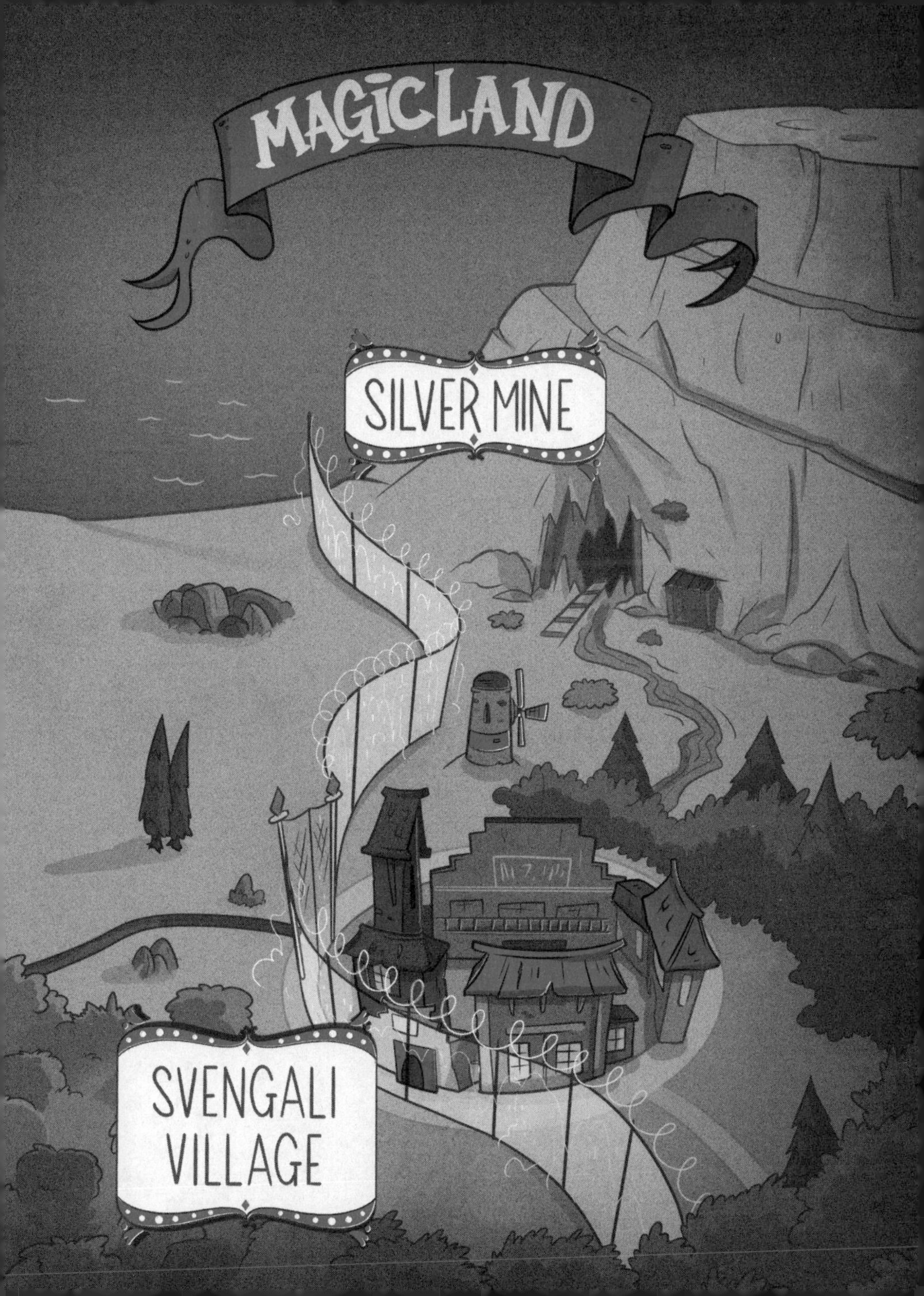
MAGICLAND
SILVER MINE
SVENGALI VILLAGE

ON ICE

"Roll up, roll up," Locki bellowed. "See the **amazing frozen man!**"

People crowded around, eyes wide. The block of ice was **frosted white** at the corners, and the sides were cloudy. But Cosentino, the Grand Illusionist, was visible inside.

"How are you doing in there, Cos?" Locki yelled.

Cos was shivering, but he winked.

"How are his vital signs?" Locki asked Priscilla.

Priscilla peered at the control panel. "His body temperature has fallen to ten degrees, but his heart rate is stable," she said, loud enough for the crowd to hear.

"Cos will emerge from this block of ice in two days," Locki announced, "at the grand opening of our **new theater**." He gestured at the building behind him, which was covered with a canvas shroud.

"**Fake**," a cat declared. "That's not ice. It's just glass."

"Perhaps you'd like to come up here and touch it?" Locki offered.

The cat approached the block of ice **warily**. She pressed her paw against the side, and yelped . . .

ME-YEOOOW!

"Satisfied?" Locki asked.

"My paw is **stuck**," she admitted.

Locki sighed. "I'll get the chisel. Again."

"Locki," Priscilla said. "His heart rate is dropping!"

Locki forgot all about the cat. "How much?" he asked.

"We're at **seventy beats per minute**. Now **sixty-five**. Now **fifty-five**!"

The crowd gathered around the control panel, trying to see. But the dials and lights were meaningless to anyone other than Priscilla and Locki.

"Cos," Priscilla cried. "Can you hear us in there?"

Cos didn't move.

Priscilla rapped on the ice. "**Concentrate**, Cos. **Focus** on your breathing. **Visualize** your heart moving your blood around, keeping your core warm."

The control panel beeped.

Locki checked. "Heart rate going back up," he said. "**He's OK!**"

The crowd cheered.

"You're overacting, Locki," Priscilla whispered.

"Nah," he replied. "They're buying it."

Cos winked again.

WARNING SIGNS

"Why am I reading about Cosentino on the front page of this **ridiculous** paper?" said the King of Diamonds. "That magician. You have to find him and get rid of him! The front page belongs to **ME**."

"Yes, your majesty," Hollow said. "As I understand it, he's doing a public performance as we speak. He often performs tricks in public. When he's not doing that, he's setting up his new theater in Coppertown. But finding him isn't the hard part.

The hard part is keeping him once we've caught him. He's an **escape artist**. He always gets away."

"I have an idea," the King said. "Round up the slaves—the ones who polish my steps. Some of them are bound to have diseases. Tell the sick ones to follow Cosentino around, **sneezing** on him. Soon he will be too ill to escape."

"Um," Hollow began. "You sent all the slaves down to the mines, my lord. It will take days to—"

"A simple fission spell should do," the King said. "Use **silver to magnify the magic** until the blast is strong enough to wipe Coppertown off the map."

The King's other head spoke up. "We don't have enough silver for a spell like that."

"Well then, **get more** from the mines, you nincompoop!" the first head said. Nincompoop was one of the King's favorite words. He liked it so much he had forbidden anyone else from using it.

"The mines produce silver very slowly," said Hollow. "As I've explained many times, the slaves you sent down there aren't actually miners. They are—"

"Silence!" The King hit Hollow with a blast of magic. Hollow's jaws **snapped shut**.

"He has a point," the King's other head said.

The King waved a hand, releasing Hollow's jaw from the spell. "Fine. What are you trying to say?"

"I know someone with knowledge of the magician and his methods," Hollow said. "His name is **Wiggy**. He claims he will be able to dispose of Cosentino without a fuss."

"Very well," the King said.

"DEPLOY WIGGY."

BACK ON ICE

The **real Cosentino** was crouched next to the giant bell in the Coppertown clock tower, watching the block of ice in the town square through binoculars.

A tapestry beside him **quivered**, **melted**, and **transformed** into Professor Camouflage.

"Is the **dummy** still fooling them?" he asked.

"Seems to be," Cos said.

MAGIC SECRET UNLOCKED

Ace had made a dummy, which looked like Cos, and frozen it in real ice. Locki had installed a mechanical eyelid and a motor in the chest, so the dummy could wink and shiver.

"What are the people in the audience saying?" the Professor asked.

"I'm not a great lip-reader, but I think Locki and Priscilla just did the **'low-heart-rate'** bit again. And the cat says her **boar** is still stuck to a block of **lice**."

"Are you sure that's right?" the Professor asked.

"She must mean her pet boar has lice. It's the only thing that makes sense."

The ice-block trick hadn't been Cos's first preference. He had wanted to do a **walking-on-water illusion**, and he had even figured out a method. He would mix cornstarch with the water so that even though still, nonmoving objects would sink, moving objects—like his feet—could bounce across the top. Unfortunately, the cornstarch would make the water look like milk, and "walking on milk" didn't have the same ring to it. So he was doing the ice trick instead.

But it was a nice change to be doing something safe. Cos's old manager, Wiggy, had always pushed him to try more and more **dangerous escapes**, with less and less rehearsal time. Cos had refused to do one particularly **risky stunt** involving a giant metal claw. Now that he was his own manager, he could decide how much danger to put himself in.

"You have your flash pots?" the Professor asked.

"Always. But I won't need them until I come out of the ice block."

"Wait a minute—you're not wearing the disguise I made for you!"

Cos shrugged. "No one can see me up here."

"Better safe than sorry," the Professor said.

Cos sighed. He took the **fake moustache** out of his pocket and stuck it to his face with a blob of magician's wax. He didn't think it was particularly convincing, but the Professor was very proud of it.

BONG!

The giant bell clanged behind them. Cos and the Professor clamped their hands over their ears. The noise was so loud it made Cos dizzy. He staggered toward the edge of the clock tower.

"Watch out!" the Professor yelled.

Cos tried to turn back, but his feet wouldn't obey his brain. He took one step onto empty air—And fell.

FREE FALL

Cos held in a **scream** as he **plummeted** toward the ground. The air blasted his face. He kept one hand on his hat so it didn't fly off.

He was falling right toward a power cable which connected the clock tower to the Coppertown library.

The cable would cut him in half!

Thinking quickly, Cos pulled off his hat and balanced his feet on the brim. It was a special magician's hat, reinforced with steel around the rim so heavy objects could be hidden inside.

He landed on the power line. The hat didn't snap. Instead, it slid down the cable like a **skateboard on a rail**, with Cos riding on top of it!

But the wall of the library was coming up fast.
Cos was about to hit it! He threw himself off the hat
and dropped down onto—

Cos scrambled off the
horse and ran away.

The horse looked back at
the driver of the carriage.
"Was that Cosentino?"
the horse asked. "The
illusionist?"

"Of course not," the driver
said. "Cosentino is sealed
in a block of ice—and he
doesn't have a moustache."

Cos gave a thumbs-up to the Professor, who was
peering anxiously over the edge of the clock tower.
It was kind of boring up there, so Cos decided to
walk through Coppertown Park before going back.

There was a lot to see. Two benches were playing musical chairs near a statue of Wanda Magellon, the master magician from long ago. Cane toads hobbled past with their walking sticks. A cricket was bowling a ball at a bat, and trees were leafing through books.

At the edge of the park, Cos crossed the street to make his way back to the clock tower. Suddenly, he heard a voice.

"Hello, young man."

Cos looked over and saw a microphone with a sack standing in a shady alley.

I'm Mike!

I'm not Cosentino.

"Would you care for some silver?" Mike asked.

"I don't have any money." Like everyone else in Coppertown, Cos was pretty much always broke.

The King made sure that the wealth of Magicland stayed in Silver City.

Mike's grin widened. "Very well. Consider it a gift."

Cos was **suspicious**, but he was also **curious**. Silver was an excellent conductor of magic, which made it the most **valuable** substance in Magicland. Who would give it away for free? **IT SOUNDED LiKe a TRiCK.** And Cos loved tricks.

"Do I know you from somewhere?" he asked as he approached the alley.

"I doubt that," Mike said. "I'm from Silver City—and you look like a Coppertowner, through and through."

He opened the sack. Inside were hundreds of **shining** silver balls.

Cos could practically feel the **magic radiating** out from the bag. Just having one of those silver balls in his pocket would give his spells a hundred times more power . . .

But spells were forbidden, so he didn't have much use for it.

"Where did you get this?" he asked.

"From the mines near Svengali Village," Mike said. "It's the source of all the **King's silver.**"

He tossed one of the silver balls to Cos, who caught it. The metal was **cold** against his palm. Then Mike closed the sack.

"Why are you giving it away?" Cos asked.

"I'm hoping to get someone's attention," Mike said. "A gentleman named Cosentino."

"Never heard of him," Cos said quickly.

"I believe you'll find him sealed in ice in Coppertown square," Mike said. "When he thaws, perhaps you could tell him about the mine."

"What about it?"

"The King is completely dependent on this mine. If **something went wrong** there—say, if all the slaves escaped—the ripples would be felt throughout Magicland. The King's hold on Coppertown might even slip." Mike coughed. "I thought Cosentino and his friends might be **interested** by this possibility."

"They might," Cos said cautiously.

"A **dance troupe** is visiting Svengali the day after tomorrow to entertain the miners. A group of **illusionists,** properly **disguised**, could take their place. I've heard this Cosentino is good at disguises."

Cos adjusted his false moustache.

Remember, silver mine. Svengali Village. The King is vulnerable right now, but he may not be for long.

Cos looked down at the ball of silver in his hand. **Could he really loosen the King's grip on Coppertown by cutting off the supply of silver?**

When he looked up, the microphone was gone.

CRASH COURSE

"You want me to teach you to dance," Princess Priscilla said doubtfully.

"Right," Cos said.

"In one day?"

"In two hours. We have to **disguise** ourselves as dancers and go to the mines tonight, so we can **sneak** in and **free the slaves** before the real dancers arrive tomorrow."

Priscilla's eyebrows went up.

"It'll be fun," Cos promised.

They were standing on the shiny wooden stage in Cos's new theater. The grand opening was tomorrow. The velvet seats would be full of creatures from all over Coppertown, eager to see him emerge from the block of ice.

"Dancing is hard," Priscilla said. "You need **BALANCE**, **FLEXIBILITY**, **strength**, a **sense of rhythm** . . . to do all of this, I took classes and practiced for years and years."

Try this!

Cos looked smug. "It might take years for a **normal** person, but—"

"I'm going to stop you before you offend me," Priscilla said. "**Try this**."

"Easy peasy," Cos said. He spun around once, twice—

And then slipped. He **crashed** headfirst onto the stage.

Priscilla looked amused. "Can you get up? Or do you need a normal person to help you?"

Cos stood, dusting himself off. "We just oiled the stage," he grumbled. "It's slippery."

"Uh-huh. Try again."

This time Cos only managed one spin before falling over. But at least he landed on his bum rather than his head.

"You're right," Priscilla said. "This **IS** fun."

"OK, I don't need to be perfect," Cos said. "I just need to be good enough to fool the guards at the village gates. Then I can get in and help the slaves escape from the mines."

"Are the guards going to ask you to dance?"

"I don't know. Maybe."

"Fine. Come here." Priscilla held out her hands. Cos took them.

"There are many different kinds of dance," Priscilla said. "There's waltzing, the cha-cha, swing dancing, line dancing, break dancing . . . I'm concerned you might literally break something break dancing, so let's start with a waltz."

She pulled Cos toward her, spinning him slowly around the room.

"One-two-three, one-two-three," she said.

"Don't make me pull you around. You're supposed to lead. That's better. Look at my face, not my feet. Big smile. Ow!"

"Sorry," Cos said. "You don't want me to step on your feet, but I also can't look at them?"

"You heard me."

"That's hard."

Priscilla released him. "Exactly. Now you understand."

Cos sighed. "So, you can't help me."

"I didn't say that." Priscilla pointed at him. "De røde sko!"

The spell **sizzled** through the air and seized control of Cos's legs. Suddenly they started hopping and kicking and **writhing like snakes**. The heels and toes of his shoes clacked on the stage.

"I'm tap-dancing!" he cried.

"Yep," Priscilla said.

"Why didn't you just do that to start with?"

"That wouldn't have been much fun."

Priscilla was the evil King's niece. She had grown up in Silver City, where spells were not illegal. Cos kept having to remind himself that magic was all about practice, and Priscilla had much more practice than him. When it came to illusions though, Cos was still the best!

"By the way, I'm coming with you," Priscilla said.

Cos looked up from his dancing legs. "You are?"

"You can dance now, but it won't be very convincing if you don't have a partner. I'm off to pack." Priscilla walked off into the stage wings.

"Can you end the dancing spell first?" Cos called. But she was gone.

Cos sighed and tap-danced his way across the stage, behind the curtain and over to the safe. **Clackety-clackety-clack**, went his feet.

The safe had a six-digit combination. It was hard to work the dial. His fingers kept shaking because of his dancing legs. If only Locki was here—he could open just about anything!

Finally Cos got the safe open, and pulled out his

illegal spell book. He turned the pages, looking for a **dancing-reversal spell**. But all he found were reverse-dancing spells, like for the moonwalk.

"You're making a lot of noise for someone who's supposed to be **hiding**," Nonna said.

"Nonna," Cos said. "Do you know any dancing-prevention spells?"

Nonna raised an eyebrow.

"I asked Priscilla to teach me to dance," Cos

explained, still dancing. "She left me like this."

"Mm-hmm. Did you insult her, possibly?"

"Maybe. I also stepped on her foot," Cos admitted.

Nonna pulled a flask out of her apron and tossed it over. Cos caught it.

"It's an anti-potion," Nonna said. "Drink some, and any enchantments will go away. But stay away from bees for two days afterward."

"Bees?"

"You heard me."

Cos **sipped the potion**. His legs went limp, and he fell over. He was getting to know his new stage very well. "You just happened to have that on you?" he asked.

"You never know," Nonna said, and winked. "Stay out of trouble, grandson."

SIGNS OF DISASTER

They had just passed a **big purple sign** which said **SVENGALI VILLAGE THIS WAY** when Snuggles yelled, "Stop!"

Priscilla hit the brakes. The car lurched to a halt.

"What?" she asked.

"I see guards."

Snuggles lived in Cos's hat. She had **amazing senses**—even for a rabbit. She could see, hear and smell better than anyone else Cos knew. This was a gift, and also a curse. If a single audience member farted during Cos's stage show, Snuggles knew about it.

Cos raised his binoculars. Snuggles was right.

The guards stood in front of a magical fence surrounding the village. The fence was **fifteen feet high**, with spelldust raining down from the **razor wire** on the top. Cos wasn't sure what the enchantment did—it was sure to be something **bad**.

The only way in was past the guards.

"Remember," said Cos's friend the Ace of Spades. "You only have one night to get the slaves out. The real dancers are due to perform tomorrow. You'll have to get out before they arrive, otherwise the guards will realize they've been tricked. Then they might summon the **JOKERS**."

Priscilla shuddered.

"Who are the **JOKERS**?" Cos asked. He hadn't seen them the last time he was sneaking into the King's palace.

Priscilla and Ace looked at each other. Priscilla

was the King's niece, and Ace had **escaped** from the King's Army of 52. They both knew more than Cos did about the King's servants.

"You don't want to know," Priscilla said finally. "Let's just make sure we get in and out quickly."

She and Cos climbed out of the car. Snuggles and Professor Camouflage followed. The Professor **transformed** himself into a cane, while Snuggles hid inside Cos's hat. Ace climbed into the driver's seat. He was their getaway driver.

"What do we tell the guards when they ask why we're a day early?" the Professor said.

"You tell them nothing," Cos said. "You're a cane, remember? Mouth shut."

"Right. Gotcha."

"Uh-oh," Snuggles said, peeping out of Cos's hat.

"What?" Cos asked.

"Someone's coming." Snuggles pointed up the road toward Silver City.

Cos looked through the binoculars.

"I smell leotards," Snuggles said.

Cos's heart sank. "The real dancers! They're here already!"

"What do we do?" Ace asked.

Cos's mind was racing. If the dancers got to Svengali Village first, he and his friends wouldn't be able to get past the guards.

"Ace," he said. "Take the Professor. Try to **get rid** of the dancers. Tell them Svengali Village is in the opposite direction."

Ace looked doubtfully at the big sign.

Svengali Village This Way →

I don't think that will work.

"Tell them something else, then. Go, go!"

The Professor **transformed** back into a lizard and leaped into the car. Ace did a U-turn and **zoomed** back toward the approaching carriage.

"What about us?" Priscilla asked.

"We'll head for the village," Cos said. "If Ace can't convince the dancers to go away, we need to get in first. That way the guards will think they're the impostors, not us."

Priscilla and Cos **sprinted** down the road toward the guards and Svengali Village.

CAR WRECK

Ace sent the car **hurtling** up the road toward the dancers' carriage.

"What's the plan?" the Professor called from the back seat.

"I have no idea," Ace said. He **flashed** his lights at the carriage. It kept coming. "They're not stopping," he said. "We have to block the road. Is your seat belt on?"

"Yes. Why do you—argh!"

Ace spun the wheel and **slammed** on the brakes, sending the car into a spin. The front wheel hit a rock and the car **flipped**, landing on one side and sliding up the road in a **shower of sparks**.

Hey, watch out!

The horse panicked and rose up on its rear legs, nearly knocking the carriage over.

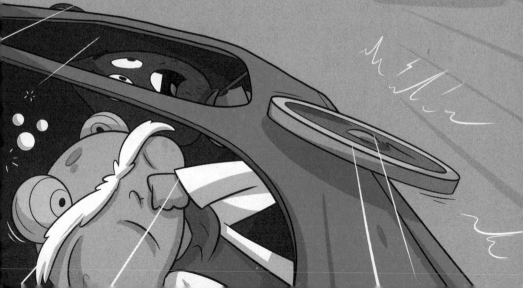

The car stopped, blocking the road. Ace had done the stunt perfectly.

Ace climbed out of the wreckage. "I'm so sorry!" he shouted.

The two dancers leaped from the carriage and struck poses.

"Are you OK?" Ace asked.

We're fabulous. But you're in the way! We're heading to an important performance in Svengali Village, and we need time to do our makeup!

"Of course." Ace pretended to try to push the car out of the way. "We're in a hurry too. We're on our way to a dance audition in Silver City."

The two dancers looked at each other.

"A dance audition, you say?" one asked.

"Yes. For a role in the royal ballot. A production of Goose Lake."

"Do you mean Swan Lake? And the royal ballet?"

"Um, yes. That's what I meant." Ace coughed. "Say, are you two dancers? You should go!"

The two dancers whispered to each other for a moment.

"We don't have time!" one hissed.

"But it's Swan Lake!" hissed the other.

"We have to go to the mines. It's the King's orders!"

"I've changed my mind," said a **booming** voice.

Ace turned around. He was **horrified** to see the King of Diamonds climbing out of the crashed car! The dancers bowed immediately.

Your majesty!

The King winked at Ace, who sighed with relief. It was only Professor Camouflage.

"The show in Svengali Village is canceled," the fake King boomed. "I was on my way to judge the auditions for Duck Lake instead when this nincompoop overturned my car."

"Swan Lake," Ace muttered.

"Silence, nincompoop!"

Ace shut up.

"Your majesty," one of the dancers stammered. "I beg you—may we audition?"

The fake King beamed. "But of course! I'll see you there, as soon as my car is fixed."

"Thank you, your majesty!" the dancers cried. Then they **jumped** into the carriage and sped back toward Silver City.

Ace exhaled. "That was close. Nice work, Professor."

"Silence, nincompoop!" the Professor commanded, but Ace ignored him.

"Soon they'll realize they've been tricked," Ace said. "Cos needs to get into that village, fast."

FALSE IDENTITY

"Halt!" the Club soldier shouted, waving his spear.

Cos and Priscilla stopped running and stuck their hands up.

Who are you?

I'm Paul McSmitherson, this is my associate, Frilly.

"You look rather like a known criminal by the name of Cosentino," the Diamond growled.

"Why, thank you," Cos said. "He's handsome."

Priscilla kicked Cos's ankle.

"That can't be right," the Club objected. "Cosentino is sealed in a block of ice in Coppertown."

"And he doesn't have a moustache," Priscilla added.

The Diamond nodded slowly. "Very well. What brings you to Svengali Village?"

"We're dancers," Cos said. "Here to perform for the miners."

"I see," the Club said suspiciously. "You know you're a day early?"

"We need to warm up," Priscilla said. "A good hamstring stretch takes six hours."

"And there's two of us," Cos added. "With four legs to stretch."

"Where's your car?"

Cos looked back up the road. He was **alarmed** to see the car lying on its side in the distance.

"Uh . . ." he said. "We seem to have crashed it."

"But never fear," Priscilla put in. "We're dancers. We have no need of props."

"If you really are dancers," the Diamond said, "you'll be able to demonstrate a yum-cha for us."

"Do you mean a cha-cha?" Cos asked.

The Diamond smiled. They had passed the test. "I'm sorry I doubted you. Welcome to Svengali Village."

The houses in Svengali Village were bigger than those in Coppertown, but just as shoddy—rotting planks holding up leaky roofs. People dragged clattering wagons up dirt roads. Some of the wagons were filled with flour from the enormous mill on top of the hill.

The King might have been mining his silver here, but apparently the locals weren't allowed to keep any of it. Flour seemed to be all they had.

"Where are all the kids?" Priscilla asked.

Cos looked around. **There were no children**. A long-abandoned playground stood nearby, the chains on the swings broken.

"Come on," Cos said, uneasy. "Let's try to find the silver mine."

They walked up the road past a grocery store, a library and a newsstand which sold magic newspapers. *The Royal Chronicle* had been **enchanted** by the King's wizards so the ink could move across the page after printing. Whenever the King changed his mind about something he said, he removed the quote from yesterday's paper and claimed he had never said it. Today's headline said, *Coppertowners still thrilled with magic ban.*

Cos was looking for a sign to the silver mine, but there was nothing. In a tiny village like this, signs weren't required. Everyone knew where everything was.

A pair of scissors walked past.

"Excuse me," Cos said.

"I'm busy," the scissors snapped. "I have a hair appointment to get to."

"We are dancers," Priscilla said, "sent by the King to perform for the miners."

The scissors **gasped**. "Sent by the King?! Forgive me. Welcome! Would you like some flour to eat?"

"No thanks," Cos said. "Can you show us to the mine?"

"Certainly! Anything for a fellow servant of our **marvelous ruler**. The mine, you say? Right this way."

They followed the scissors around the corner of the newsstand, where the dirt road narrowed to a muddy trail as it approached a forest. The scissors kept **babbling** the whole way. "You said you were dancers? How wonderful. What an honor, to perform on the King's orders. I'm a performer

myself, you know. A razor, a comb and I have a
barbershop quartet." The scissors handed Cos a
polaroid. "There's only three of us, but I'm a pair,
you see."

"Thanks," Cos said. "Before you go, can I ask you a question?"

"Certainly!" the scissors said.

"Where are all the children?" Cos hadn't seen any in the village.

The scissors looked **worried**. "Right where they're supposed to be!" she said. "And if you hear otherwise, it's a lie."

She ran back up the dirt trail toward Svengali Village, as if she was **running for her life**.

"Is it me," Cos asked, "or was that very **weird**?"

"It's not you," Priscilla said. She gestured at the mine. "Shall we go in?"

Cos looked at the foreboding shadows. "I guess we should. I didn't bring a flashlight, though." He had his flash pots. When activated they made a **bright light** and **puff of smoke**, but the light

73

only lasted a second or two, and the smoke would make it even harder to see.

Priscilla held out her hand. "**WENZULSTEIN**!" she whispered. A **ball of fire** appeared, hovering above her palm. Spelldust trickled between her fingers and rained down on the mud.

"If Hollow turns up," Cos said, "he'll be able to smell the spelldust."

"Then we'd better be quick."

Cos took a deep breath, and walked into the darkness of the mine.

WATCH YOUR STEP

The mine was dark, but it wasn't silent. Cos could hear the **clattering** of wheels, the **banging** of tools and **shouting** voices.

Not adult voices, though. Children.

"I think we've found the missing kids," he said. "They're the King's slaves."

They trudged deeper and deeper into the tunnel. Even with the flickering fire in Priscilla's hand, they couldn't see much. The ceiling got lower and lower until they had to stoop. When they got to a T-intersection, they stopped.

"Which way are the voices coming from?" Cos asked.

"I can't tell."

A **muffled** voice came out of Cos's hat. "I can."

"Snuggles!" Cos said. "I forgot you were with us."

"As usual," Snuggles said. She popped out of Cos's hat and pointed.

If you're hoping to rescue the kids, they're that way!

Cos started walking. "Thanks, Snuggles."

"You're welcome. Watch out for the underground lake."

"What underground—

AaaaaRRGH!"

It was like landing in an **ice bath**. Cos barely held in a scream as the freezing water shot up his nose and flooded his ears. It soaked his clothes and he immediately started to sink.

Cos was a strong swimmer, but the cold had shocked his muscles. His arms and legs were already **going numb**. He kept expecting his kicking feet to touch the bottom, but they didn't. The lake was deep. He was going to drown!

Through the rippling surface of the water, he saw Priscilla throw her **fireball** down at the lake. It **streaked** toward him like an asteroid.

The fireball hit the lake.

The water around Cos turned into a **cloud of vapor**. An invisible force squeezed him as Priscilla lifted him out of the water with a levitation spell.

He floated back toward Priscilla, and then the spell released him. He collapsed to the floor, shivering.

"You OK?" Priscilla asked.

"Yeah," Cos said. "Snuggles? A bit more warning next time, please."

There was no answer from inside his hat, but he could hear the **whining of a hair dryer**. Snuggles was probably drying her fur.

"How are we going to get across?" Priscilla asked. "I can't levitate both of us at the same time."

Cos was about to reply when he heard something. The lapping of water against the sides of a boat.

"**SoMEoNE'S CoMiNG**," he whispered.

TRICKERY

Cos and Priscilla ducked out of sight behind a stalagmite just in time. The rowboat materialized out of the **gloom**.

"I don't see anybody," a voice said. It sounded like a young boy.

"I'm telling you, I heard a splash," someone else said. A girl.

"Could have been sharks."

"We've been over this—there are no sharks. The

King **lied**, to stop us from swimming across the lake."

"Oh yeah? Then who ate Ben?"

"There is no Ben. The King made him up too."

These people didn't sound like bad guys, so Cos stood up. "Hello there!" he called.

Sudden silence.

As the boat drifted into view, Cos saw the occupants.

They weren't kids. They were older than Cos— older than Nonna, even.

A man and a woman with gray hair, stooped backs and deep wrinkles in their skin.

Cos coughed with surprise. "Pardon me, sir and madam," he said, when he recovered. "I thought you were children."

"We are children," the old man said. "Who are you?"

"Uh, my name is Cosentino," Cos said. He didn't reveal Priscilla, just in case. "I'm here to help you."

"Do you, uh, work for the King?" the old man asked Cos.

"No," Cos said. "I'm an illusionist. I'm here to free the miners."

"That's us. But how do we know this isn't some kind of trick?"

"Check this out." Cos pulled a small black box out of his pocket and removed a cube. It was

about the size of a die, but the sides had colors instead of numbers.

He **tossed** the cube and the box to the people in the the boat. Then he turned his back.

"Examine the objects, then put the cube back in the box with your chosen color facing up," he said. "Close the lid so I can't see it."

"Done," the old woman said.

"Great." Cos turned around. "Now give the box back to me."

She tossed it over. Cos caught the box and held it behind his back, without breaking eye contact with the old woman.

"I want you to **think of your color,**" he said.

"The one which was facing up. Imagine the word for the color **hanging in the air**, right in front of me. Are you doing that?"

"Yes," the old woman said uncertainly.

Cos held the box up in one hand. With the other, he started tracing a **shape in the air**.

A backward letter. *R*.

"No way," the old man whispered.

Cos traced out two more backward letters: *E* and *D*. *Red*.

"How did you . . ." the old woman said.

Cos pocketed the box. "*That* **was a trick**," he said. "*This* **is a rescue**. Can we hop in the boat?"

"We?"

"Oh, right." Cos took off his coat and held it up next to him. Priscilla crept from behind the rock to behind the coat, and stood up. Cos dropped the coat, revealing her.

"Ta-da!" Priscilla said.

The two sailors' eyes widened.

"Well," the old woman said. "Obviously they are illusionists."

"That doesn't mean we should trust them," the old man said.

"No," the old woman agreed. "But how much worse could things get?" She held out a hand. "Welcome aboard."

The Missing Mine

The journey across the lake was long and spooky. The black water was like a mirror beneath them, revealing nothing under the surface. Sometimes the boat had to steer around huge stalagmites which towered above them like stone trees.

The old woman had introduced herself as Spin. The old man was Russ.

"We used to live in Svengali Village," Spin said. "But then the King's soldiers kidnapped us and took us to Silver City. We spent a few months polishing the palace steps. Then he sent us back to the village. We thought we were going home. But instead, he made us come down here. Once per day we load up all the silver and take it across the lake—"

"The **SHARK-INFESTED LAKE**," Russ put in.

"The *allegedly* shark-infested lake. Then the **JOKERS** pick it up, and leave some food behind for us to take back."

Priscilla shuddered.

"We've been down here for . . ." Spin hesitated. "What do you reckon, Russ? Six months?"

"It's hard to tell without daylight," Russ said. "The food deliveries are the only way of measuring the days."

For a moment, the only sound was the lapping

of the water against the sides of the boat.

"Have you ever tried to escape?"

"Once," Spin said. "But there are fifty of us, and only one little boat. The lake is **too big** and **too cold** to swim across. And Wiggy would notice if—"

"Did you say 'Wiggy'?" Cos asked.

"Yeah. He's the boss down here."

A **sense of doom** was creeping up on Cos. Why was his old manager working in a silver mine?

"Don't worry," Priscilla said. "We're going to get you out of here. All of you."

The boat stopped suddenly. It had reached the edge of the lake and run aground. Beyond there were more tunnels, with tracks and mine carts. Loudspeakers were mounted on the stone walls.

"Come on," Russ said. "We'll introduce you to the others."

As they splashed across the water toward the shore, Priscilla tapped Cos on the shoulder. They both fell behind so they could talk privately.

"They talk like kids," she said. "But they look ancient."

"I know. But it's pretty dark down here. Maybe we'll figure out what the deal is once we've gotten them up to the surface. Could you try your teleporting spell?"

"There's iron in the rock," Priscilla said. "I can feel it. The kids might get stuck halfway."

Cos nodded slowly. Magic and iron didn't mix.

"That's problem number one," Priscilla said. "Problem number two: we're directly beneath Svengali Village."

"So even if we got up there, we'd still be trapped within the magic fence."

If magic can't get us out of here, Cos thought, *maybe an illusion can.*

Some other people emerged from the darkness. But as they greeted Spin and Russ, they sounded young, like kids.

"Can you get us out of here?" Jonesy asked.

"Please?" Mill added.

"I think so," Cos said. "I'll just need some equipment. What kinds of tools do you use to dig the holes?"

"Holes?" Russ looked puzzled.

"Yeah. Do you have **explosive charges**?" Cos had his flash pots, but they had very little explosive power. They wouldn't work for what he had in mind.

"What holes?" Spin asked.

Now it was Cos's turn to look **puzzled**. "Aren't you guys the miners?"

"Oh," Spin said. "I get it. We're not miners, we're *minors*. You know, kids."

THE MiNORS

King's slaves/miners
Silver Mine
Abilities: Being minors

96

"The King made the same mistake," Russ put in. "He assumed we'd be good at mining because he didn't understand the difference between minors and miners."

"But . . . you're old," Cos said.

Spin and Russ looked at each other and sighed.

"I'm eleven," Spin said. "He's nine. We look like this because we used to polish the steps in Silver City all day long. The **shiny silver** and the **mirrored walls** of the city made the sun so intense that it **bleached our hair** and made us all **wrinkly**."

"Oh. I'm sorry." Cos remembered seeing some old people polishing the King's steps. It was shocking to think that they had been younger than him.

Wait, he thought. *If they're not doing any mining, then where is the silver coming from?*

"Get all the others together," Priscilla told the kids. "We want to be out of here before the **JOKERS** come."

They all nodded eagerly, and ran off.

The loudspeakers crackled and whined:

"This is an important message from the King of Diamonds: work harder. End of message."

Cos leaned on a mine cart, which appeared to be filled with birdseed. "So," he said. "How are we going to—"

"Thank goodness you came!" a voice boomed.

Cos **squinted** into the darkness. Someone was approaching from a nearby tunnel. Someone familiar. It was Mike—the microphone who had given him the silver ball in Coppertown.

"Hello again," Cos said.

"You must be Princess Priscilla," Mike said. "Tales of your derring-do have spread throughout Magicland. It's an **honor**."

"The honor is mine." Priscilla looked at Cos for an explanation.

"This is Mike," Cos said. "The guy who told me about the mine."

"Come this way," Mike said. "I have something to show you."

Cos and Priscilla followed the microphone through a dark, narrow tunnel. Cos had to breathe in so he could **squeeze** through some of the gaps.

The tunnel led to an iron gate next to a rusty lever. They walked through the gate and found themselves in a long chamber. A portrait of the evil King was on the wall. An old mining scoop dangled from the ceiling like a **claw in an arcade machine.** Rope was everywhere, coiled in the corners and trailing across the floor. Cos wondered if they could use it to climb out somehow.

But then he got distracted by something else. At the far end of the chamber stood a **T-shaped metal bar**. And sitting atop it was . . .

"A pigeon?" Priscilla asked, confused.

It did look a bit like a pigeon. But as Cos got closer, he realized that its feathers weren't gray. They were just dirty.

It's a dove," Cos said. He patted it gently. The dove **cooed**.

Both the bird's ankles were chained to the T-bar. That explained why it hadn't flown out of this awful place.

"Poor thing," Cos said. "I wonder—"

Then he spotted something. On the floor beneath the dove was a **silver ball**, just like the ones Mike had showed him.

DOVE

King's Silver Layer
Silver Mine
Abilities: Lays Eggs of Silver

An egg . . .

I don't get it.

"This is where the silver is coming from," Cos said. "They're not mining it. The King has a dove which **lays silver eggs**. He's keeping it prisoner down here." *That explains the mine cart filled with birdseed*, he thought.

"So if we free it, along with the kids," Priscilla said, "that will cut off his supply of silver."

Cos turned around in time to see the iron gate swing shut.

Mike had **locked** them in the chamber!

REVENGE

Before Cos could run over to the gate, something **gripped** his foot. He looked down. One of the loops of rope on the floor had **tightened** itself around his ankle.

Priscilla **screamed** as the rope dragged Cos off his feet and pulled him into the air, making him drop the silver egg. Now he was **hanging upside down**, right beneath the clawlike mining scoop. Everything fell out of his pockets.

SPONGE
BALLS

YO-YO

FLASH
POTS

This all seemed horribly familiar. He looked through the gate in time to see Mike the microphone put on a wig. Now he looked just like someone Cos used to know . . .

WIGGY

MINE OVERSEER/COS'S OLD MANAGER
ABILITIES: BEING BOSSY AND CUNNING

"Mike, you're **Wiggy**!" Cos cried.

"At last," Wiggy said. "I thought you'd never recognize your old manager."

The blood was rushing to Cos's head. The **pressure** hurt his skull. "Wiggy," he said, "don't do this."

"It was so easy," Wiggy said, rubbing his hands together with glee. "When the King told me to catch you, I summoned the dancers to the mine. Then I found you and told you about the slaves. I knew you wouldn't be able to resist. Now the **JOKERS** are on their way and you're caught in my trap."

Who are you? What do you want?

I used to work for Cos. We made a great team. But—

"You could have gotten me **killed**, Wiggy," Cos said. "That escape was too dangerous."

"After Cos **fired** me," Wiggy continued, "I could only get a job working for the King. My salary isn't even enough to pay the rent."

"I'm sorry that happened to you, Wiggy," Cos said. "But—"

"I just kept thinking about that last escape," Wiggy continued. "The one with the claw. The one you said was **too dangerous**. Were you **right**, or were you just being a **coward**? Now we're going to find out."

"Your problem is with me," Cos said.

"LET PRISCILLA GO!"

"I intend to. Just as soon as you've attempted the stunt." Wiggy put his hand on a lever next to the iron gate. "One minute after I pull this lever, that claw will **snap shut**, breaking every bone in your body. You have **sixty seconds** to untie the rope and get out of the way." He grinned. "Either you **survive**, and the trick wasn't dangerous after all . . . or you were **right!**"

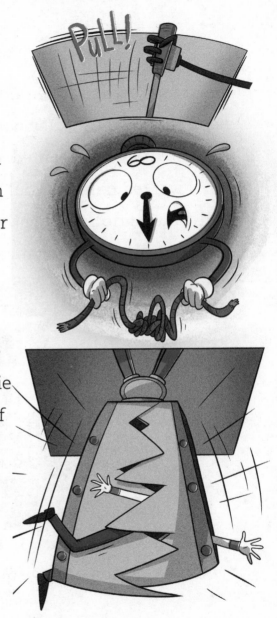

Cos's heart was **racing**. "I'm happy to do dangerous escapes," he said, "but on my terms. I need rehearsal time. It's not fair to—"

"Fair?!" Wiggy screamed. "I'll tell you what's not fair. I worked hard for you! We could have made **millions of dollars** together. Frankly, I hope you were right about how dangerous this stunt was."

I want to see you crushed!

He pulled the lever.

Above Cos, something started to **tick**.

Sixty Seconds of Danger

While Wiggy had been talking, Cos had been **wriggling** his ankles around, trying to loosen the ropes. He'd had no success. The rope was thick and strong, and tight enough to bruise his skin.

Cos **folded** his body at the hips, trying to untie the rope with his hands. He knew hundreds of knots, but most of them were trick knots, which seemed very sturdy unless the right end was pulled in just the right way.

113

This wasn't a trick knot. It was as complex as **SPAGHETTI** and as hard as a **ROCK**.

> Priscilla! Find me something to land on!

Priscilla dragged over some of the other ropes and heaped them in a pile.

It wouldn't be a soft landing, but it would be better than the stone floor.

But not if Cos couldn't untie his feet. And the knots refused to loosen.

The claw **TiCK-TiCK-TiCKeD** above him, hidden mechanisms counting away the seconds, waiting to strike.

"I can't get it undone," he yelled. "Can you use **MAGIC** to stop the claw?"

"It's made of iron!" Priscilla cried. "Spells won't work!" She scrabbled around on the ground until she found a metal bar. One end was jagged—it looked like it might have broken off something.

"Here—just cut the rope!" She tossed the bar up into the air. Cos caught it and started sawing at the rope.

"Hey! That's cheating!" Wiggy bellowed. He jiggled the lever, but he couldn't make the claw close any faster.

The broken end of the bar was too blunt to cut the rope. Maybe Cos could **jam the claw open** instead. He tried to wedge the bar into the mechanism.

But it didn't work. The bar was **too big** to fit into the hinge, and **too small** to brace the claws apart.

"**LESS THAN TEN SECONDS LEFT,**" Wiggy cackled.

Cos looked around. There was nothing else he could use. He was doomed.

"Keep trying!" Priscilla cried.

Cos looked back at the knot. But it was too late. There was no way he could get it undone.

Until . . .

"**FIREBALL!**" Priscilla yelled, and she picked up the silver dove egg and threw it at Cos.

Cos understood her plan.

WENZULSTEIN!

Cos caught
the silver ball, which
channeled his magic
into a **strong spell**.
A fireball appeared in Cos's
hand, and he **flung** it at the
rope. The flames danced
across the fibers.

THE TIMER WENT OFF.

60

DING!

CLUNK!

Cos had **plummeted** through the chamber and crashed safely down onto the pile of ropes.

"We did it!" Priscilla crowed.

Cos high-fived her, and turned to face Wiggy.

"I knew you could do it. Traitorous trickster! To think, all of these years I could have been rich . . . well it doesn't matter now," Wiggy snarled.

"THE JOKERS ARE HERE! REVENGE IS MINE!"

No Laughing Matter

Cos could hear a noise in the tunnel, getting closer and closer. It sounded like **squeaking wheels**. And laughter.

All the color drained from Priscilla's face. "The **JOKERS** are here!" she cried. "What do we do?"

Cos picked his stuff up off the floor. "Can you open the gate? With magic?"

Priscilla **blasted** a spell at the gate. It didn't move at all. Like the claw, it was made of iron.

Escape!
Escape!

How?

"Escape!" the dove insisted. She jerked her beak toward the corner of the chamber.

As Cos looked closely, he noticed something. It was almost completely hidden under the piles of rope, but it looked like—

"An escape hatch!" he cried.

Priscilla started clearing the rope away so they could get to the **trapdoor**.

Cos pulled a bobby pin out of his hair and got to work on the **chains** around the dove's ankles. The locks were too complex for a dove to pick, but not for a trained illusionist.

Let him try.

Priscilla had cleared the trapdoor. Cos **ran** over to help her lift it. Underneath it they found a narrow, horizontal **tunnel**, pitch black.

The walls were worn smooth. It looked like it had been used for water drainage.

Cos and Priscilla crawled in. The dove followed. Cos pulled the trapdoor shut behind them, hoping Wiggy wouldn't be able to lift it by himself.

The tunnel split into two. Then it split again, and again. Each time, Cos and Priscilla followed the dove. She seemed to know where she was going.

Then she **FROZE**.

Cos and Priscilla froze too. Something was coming.

LAUGHTER echoed through the tunnels. The **JOKERS** were down here.

"Follow," the dove whispered. She changed direction and led them up another tunnel.

Soon Cos heard kids' voices, and then they

emerged into a cavern which had dozens of
sleeping mats rolled out on the stone. The kids
were in there, playing hockey with a rock.

"We had a run-in with Wiggy," Cos said. "Now the **JOKERS** are here. We have to get out of the mine, now."

Spin's eyes were **wide with fear**.

They're on this side of the lake?

Yes. We need to get across to the other side, fast.

How? We only have one boat!

"I have an idea." Cos pulled the **silver egg** and one of the **flash pots** out of his pocket. "Priscilla, can you use the silver to enchant this flash pot?"

"To do what?"

"I want it to **explode**," Cos said. "Not just smoke and light—I want an actual kaboom."

"Sure," Priscilla said. "**ABRA KABOOMRA!**"

The flash pot started to **glow** in Cos's hand.

"It's gonna blow in about sixty seconds," Priscilla said. "I hope you have a plan."

"I do," Cos said. "Try to teleport it into the **flour mill** in Svengali Village."

"There's too much iron above us. The flash pot will get stuck in the ceiling."

"That's the idea."

"But why . . ." Priscilla trailed off.

"You see what I'm getting at?" Cos asked.

"I do. It might just be **crazy** enough to work."

"What are you two talking about?" Spin demanded.

"A magic trick," Cos said.

"EVERYBODY, FOLLOW ME!"

131

HELP FROM ABOVE

It was hard for fifty kids to move silently. The sound of their footsteps bounced off the walls, and their heavy breathing echoed noisily. Cos was sure the **JOKERS** had heard them, and that they would catch up at any second.

Soon the minors, Cos, Priscilla and the dove reached the lake. The dark water lapped at the muddy shore.

"Now what?" Russ asked.

Priscilla pointed at the craggy ceiling above the lake. "I think that's about where the mill was," she said.

"Give it a try," Cos said, still holding the glowing flash pot.

"**HUDU GURU!**" Priscilla said. Magic flashed out of her hands. The flash pot vanished.

Spelldust and silence fell.

"Did it work?" Cos asked.

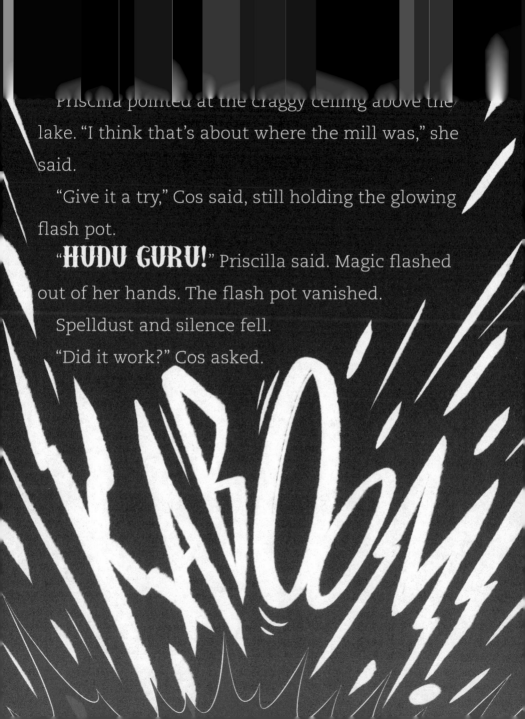

Part of the ceiling **exploded**. Hundreds of tons of flour spilled through the hole, tumbling into the lake like an **avalanche**.

"We need to **mix** it in," Cos said. He grabbed the oars from the boat and started splashing the water. It was **useless**. The flour was too far away.

"I'll use a mixing spell," Priscilla said. "**ABRACADEEJAY!**"

"OK," Cos told the kids. "We need to run across the lake. Don't stop, no matter what. If you do, you'll sink."

"Run across?" Spin said, incredulous.

"Just trust me," Cos said, hoping that the trick would work. It had worked at his theater, but **stage magic** wasn't always reliable out in the **real world**.

"There they are!" a voice shrieked.

Cos turned. Wiggy was standing in the mouth of the tunnel, pointing at the kids.

Behind him were two **monkeys**. In jester outfits. Riding unicycles.

"Oh, no!" Priscilla cried. "**THE JOKERS!**"

JOKE'S ON YOU

One Joker wore a purple shirt. The other was in white. As Cos watched, there was a **puff of spelldust**, and—

Nothing happened.

No, wait. Cos's eyes narrowed. The purple Joker was now on the white Joker's unicycle. The two monkeys had **switched places**, magically. But if that was their power, what harm could it do?

"What are you doing?" Cos hissed.

"The **JOKERS** are **naughty**," Priscilla whispered back. "They never do what you tell them."

THE JOKERS

THE KING'S JESTERS
ABILITIES: NAUGHTY, PLACE SWITCHERS

Sure enough, the white-shirted monkey leaped off the unicycle and started climbing up the wall toward the ceiling, **giggling**. But the other monkey pedaled toward the minors.

"Run!" Priscilla screamed. **"DON'T LET IT TOUCH YOU!"**

The kids started **dashing** toward the water. But it was too late. The purple monkey **grabbed** Russ by the collar.

"Let go of me!" Russ cried, struggling.

And then the two **JOKERS** magically switched places again. Now the purple monkey was **hanging from the ceiling** . . . still holding Russ!

"Help me!" screamed Russ, who was now **dangling** high above the ground.

The purple monkey **cackled** with delight . . .

Then it dropped him.

Cos sprinted toward Russ, but there was no way he'd get there in time to catch him. Russ screamed as he **plummeted** toward the tracks—

The tracks!

Cos changed direction, and barged into the mine cart. It lurched into motion, gaining speed as it rattled down the tracks toward Russ.

CRASH! Russ landed right in the cart, showering birdseed everywhere. He **scrambled** out of the cart and hit the ground, letting the cart roll away into the darkness.

Cos caught up to Russ. "Come on," he yelled, pulling the boy to his feet.

Wiggy ran up to them, furious—

But Priscilla hit one of the loudspeakers with a blast of magic.

ARGH! Feedback!

Cos and Russ **sprinted** back toward the shore. The purple **JOKER** had climbed farther across the ceiling and was now hanging above the lake. But where was the white-clad monkey?

"NO!" Cos cried.

Too late. There was an **explosion** of spelldust,

and suddenly Cos found himself **hanging** from the ceiling, high above the lake. The two **JOKERS** had switched again!

Cos was still in the **Joker's** grip. "Whatever you do," he said, "**don't drop me!**"

The naughty monkey **guffawed**, and let him go.

Cos fell, faster and faster toward the dark water . . .

And landed on top of it. Immediately he started sprinting across the water toward the other side of the lake. It felt like **running on a trampoline**.

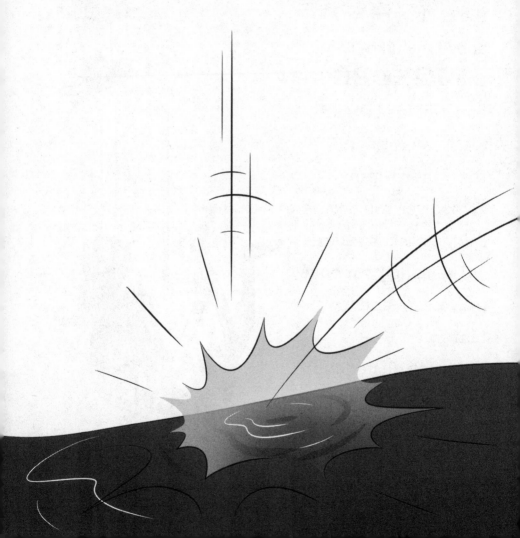

The flour had worked perfectly! But Cosentino couldn't stop, or he would start to sink.

Everybody run!

WALKING ON WATER

Wiggy watched, perplexed, as Cosentino dashed across the lake. *Impossible!*

The kids all started **sprinting** toward the lake. There was nowhere else to go. So the kids ran toward the water—

And kept running. Just like Cosentino, they weren't sinking. They sprinted across the water as though it was solid. The dove **flapped** after them, grinning.

Wiggy stared. What was going on?

The **JOKERS** gave chase. But they weren't as fast as the kids.

They hesitated at the edge of the lake, baffled.

"What are you waiting for?" Wiggy screamed.
"Get after them!"

Cautiously, the **JOKERS** stepped forward.
But they were moving too slowly, and their feet
sank right into the lake.

Screeching with horror, they tried to lift their feet out again, but it was as if they were mired in quicksand.

They swapped places.

Then they did it again.

And again.

It didn't help—both monkeys were **stuck**.

Wiggy **stared** after the disappearing kids. How could this be happening?

He approached the lake and bent down to touch it. The water wasn't water. **IT HAD A GLUEY CONSISTENCY, LIKE THIN HONEY.**

The fluid made a **SUCKING** sound as Wiggy pulled out his hand. He tried to shake it dry, but the slime stuck to his fingers.

Wiggy ran over to the rowboat and pushed it onto the lake. Then he jumped in.

The boat didn't sink. So far so good. Whatever Cos had done to the water, it hadn't affected the boat. Wiggy **jammed** the oars into the lake and tried to row.

The oars wouldn't move at all. The lake water was **much too thick**. And without any silver eggs to boost his spells, Wiggy was trapped.

ESCAPE

When Cos, Priscilla, the dove and the kids made it out of the mine, they found Ace and Professor Camouflage waiting at the entrance.

"Are these the **miners**?" the Professor asked, looking doubtfully at the crowd of **oldified** kids climbing out of the tunnel.

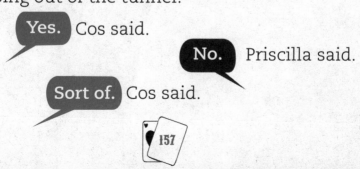

Yes. Cos said.

No. Priscilla said.

Sort of. Cos said.

157

"We're **minors**," Spin said, which only added to the confusion.

"Do we have a way out of here?" Cos asked.

"We **snuck** past the guards," the Professor said. "But I don't think we can pull it off again. Not with fifty people."

"I can **dig a tunnel** under the magic fence," said a voice from inside Cos's hat.

It was Snuggles. She popped her head out and smiled.

"Of course!" Cos said. "Why didn't we do that on the way in?"

"Beats me," Snuggles said. "Let's go!"

"We have to hurry," Ace said, as everyone followed Snuggles into the tunnel she was digging at **alarming speed**. "Cos, you're due to emerge from the block of ice in less than an hour."

Cos gasped. He had forgotten about his big trick. It hadn't seemed very important compared to rescuing the kids . . . but now that they were free, **HiS GRAND iLLUSiONS WERE ONCE AGAiN THE MOST IMPORTANT THING iN THE WORLD.**

"OK. When we get back, I need a bucket of water and some of Nonna's face cream," he said. "And Professor? I need you to **MAKE ANOTHER DiSGUiSE** for someone."

THE FOUNTAIN OF YOUTH

Locki was trying to entertain the audience at Cos's new theater.

The audience stared.

"Oh." Locki coughed. "Just a second."

He shuffled nervously through the cards again.

Every seat in the new theater was full, and people were standing in the aisles. Kids were sitting on the floor. Everyone had come to see Cosentino **emerge from the block of ice**.

Some of the people in the crowd had even helped carry the ice from the town square to the stage, which had created even more suspense.

But now the ice was slowly **melting** and Locki was trying to stall the audience.

Unfortunately, card tricks were not Locki's thing. If the real Cos didn't turn up soon, the dummy would be **exposed**, and the audience would realize how the ice trick worked.

Locki tried again. "Is this your card?"

"No," the teapot said again.

BANG!
HISS!

There was a bright flash, and the ice block turned into a cloud of steam.

A figure emerged from the fog . . .

"IT'S COSENTINO!" someone yelled.

Cos stepped forward, off the hidden trapdoor. He was **soaking wet**, and shivering. He pulled a card out of his pocket.

"I believe this is your card," he told the teapot.

The teapot took it, amazed.

MAGIC SECRET UNLOCKED

Cos had been watching from the wings, and he'd seen the teapot's card. He pocketed the same card from a spare deck, went under the stage, tipped some water on himself and activated his last flash pot. The block of ice had fallen through the trapdoor as Cos climbed out.

Locki hugged Cos, and ran off the stage.

"Ladies and gentlemen," Cos boomed. "Boys and girls, forks and spoons, hawks and moons,

WELCOME TO THE BRAND-NEW COPPERPOT THEATER!"

The white-haired, wrinkly kids from the mine shuffled into the back of the theater, grinning. Cos saw them.

"For my next trick," he said. "I'll need some volunteers. Really old volunteers." He pointed. "How about you all?"

The minors hurried up to the stage. It was barely big enough to fit them all.

"Nonna!" Cos called.

Nonna hobbled onto the stage. "Yes, grandson?"

"How is it that you always look so **incredibly youthful?**" Cos asked sweetly.

Nonna grinned. "I have a **magic potion.**"

"Oh yes? What is it called?"

"'Moisturizing cream,'" said Nonna.

"Can I borrow some?" Cos asked.

"Sure thing." Nonna tossed him a bottle.

Cos started dabbing the cream on the faces of the old people. Their wrinkles **disappeared**, and the **color** returned to their hair.

The crowd gasped.

Nonna hobbled off the stage.

"I wasn't kidding about how young she looks," Cos said, as he kept working on the kids. "She's actually five hundred and twelve!"

But then . . .

BooM!

The theater doors crashed open . . .

THE FINAL CHAPTER

Hollow **stormed** into the Copperpot Theater. The King of Diamonds was right behind him, flanked by soldiers from the Army of 52.

Hollow pointed at Cosentino. "Arrest that man!" he ordered.

The soldiers started **pushing** through the crowd toward the stage.

Cos looked perplexed. "Me? What have I done?"

"Don't play innocent!" Hollow cried.

174

"This morning, you broke into my silver mine," the King said. "And you **stole my dove!** And my slaves!"

"This morning?" Cos said. "I've been sealed in a **block of ice** for a week."

It's true.

Yeah, I was watching him the whole time.

The King looked even angrier. "I know it was you," he snarled. "Where are my slaves?"

Cos scanned the crowd. "I have no idea. What do they look like?"

"You know perfectly well what they look like!" Hollow snapped. "Old! With **white hair** and **wrinkles!**"

177

Cos gestured at all the nervous-looking kids on the stage. "I don't see any old people here," he said.

The King's soldiers were searching the room.

"Where are they?" the King demanded.

"We've found nothing, sir," one of the soldiers

said finally.

Cos shrugged. "Like I said, I was **frozen** the whole time. You've got the wrong guy."

The King's eyes narrowed. "Well, maybe you didn't do this," he said. "But I know you're up to something. I'll be **watching** you."

Cos beamed. "Great! I like to have an audience."

With a final **snarl**, the King snapped his fingers.

The soldiers retreated back into the dark.

"Sorry for the interruption, everybody," Cos said.
"Who wants to see another illusion?"

The crowd **cheered**.

Priscilla and Locki watched from the wings as
Cos brought his new **shadow box** onto the stage.

"It's funny, isn't it?" Priscilla marveled. "Cos keeps so many **secrets**, and he spends so much time alone, practicing tricks in front of a mirror. And yet, when you put him in front of a crowd, he can talk to them and make them as excited as he is. It's almost . . . **MAGICAL**."

"Maybe he has powers so **secret** he doesn't even know about them," Locki suggested.

Maybe we all do, Priscilla thought, looking at all the **smiling** faces in the audience.

"Do you think the King will come after us again?" Locki asked.

"Probably," Priscilla said. "But against you, me, Cos, Ace, Snuggles, the Professor, Nonna and fifty or so kids, the King doesn't stand a chance. Not without the **JOKERS** and his silver. He's **powerless**."

"But what if he finds the dove?"

"He won't."

"How can you be sure?"

"The Professor has made a **disguise** for her . . ."

You can learn Cos's trick from page 87!

THE VISION BOX
MAGIC TRICK INSTRUCTIONS

REQUIRED ITEMS:

A box with a lid

A cube with different colors on each side, that fits inside the box

Note: download the do-it-yourself box, lid and cube from here: www.friends.kanemiller.com

METHOD:

1. Pass both the cube and the box to a volunteer for examination.

2. Tell the volunteer to place the cube in the box with their chosen color facing up. Ask them to replace the lid and hand you the box while your back is turned. **FiG. 1**.

FiG. 1

3. When the box is in your hands (**FiG. 2**), turn around and face the volunteer, keeping the box behind you.

FiG. 2

4. Secretly take off the lid and place it on the side of the box, so the color chosen by the volunteer is revealed. **FiG. 3**.

FiG. 3

5. Bring the box in front of you, making sure that the open side is facing you and that the lid is on what appears to be the top of the box. **FiG. 4**.

FiG. 4

6. Pretend to be in deep thought, but really you can secretly glance at the box to see which color is showing. **FiG. 5**.

FiG. 5

7. Place the box behind your back again and put the lid back to its correct position. **FiG. 6**.

FiG. 6

8. Place the box on the table.

9. Act dramatically and name the chosen color. You can even pretend you are reading their mind! Then ask for the box to be opened. As if by magic you are right! **FiG. 7**.

FiG. 7

COSENTINO is now regarded as one of the world's leading magicians and escape artists. He is a multiple winner of the prestigious Merlin Award (the Oscar for international magicians) and is the highest-selling live act in his home country, Australia.

Cosentino's four prime-time TV specials have aired in over 40 countries and he has toured his award-winning live shows to full houses across the world.

JACK HEATH is a bestselling, award-winning Australian author of thrillers and used to be a street magician!

JAMES HART is an Australian children's illustrator who has illustrated many books.

Photo credit: Pierre Baroni